Scarecrow

Witch of the North

Wicked Witch of the West

Tin Woodman

The Wonderful Wizard of Oz

Dear rodent readers,
My love for great stories began a long time ago, when I was still a young mouselet. I spent hours and hours reading wonderful books! They took me on fantastic adventures to mysterious, faraway lands. Reading made my imagination soar — and it made me want to become a writer, too!

So I thought I'd share one of my very favorite tales with you — a great literary mousterpiece. I can't wait to tell you the fabumouse story of Dorothy and her friends: her dog Toto, the Scarecrow, the Tin Woodman, and the Cowardly Lion. Together, they go on an extraordinary journey to find the Wizard of Oz, hoping he'll grant them each a wish. But when they finally reach him, they discover that their adventure is just beginning!

Geronimo Stilton

Published by Scholastic Inc., *Publishers since 1920*, 557 Broadway, New York, NY 10012. SCHOLASTIC and associated logos are trademarks and/ or registered trademarks of Scholastic Inc.

Stilton is the name of a famous English cheese. It is a registered trademark of the Stilton Cheese Makers' Association. For more information, go to www.stiltoncheese.com.

This book is a work of fiction. Names, characters, places, and incidents are either the product of the author's imagination or are used fictitiously, and any resemblance to actual persons, living or dead, business establishments, events, or locales is entirely coincidental.

978-1-338-05295-4

Original text by L. Frank Baum
Adapted by Geronimo Stilton
Original title *Il meraviglioso mago di Oz*
Cover by Flavio Ferron
Illustrations by Danilo Loizedda (pencil and ink) and Edwin Nori (color)
Graphics by Silvia Bovo and Yuko Egusa

Special thanks to Shannon Penney
Translated by Emily Clement
Interior design by Becky James

10 9 8 7 6 5 4 3 2 1   16 17 18 19 20

Printed in the U.S.A.   40
First printing 2016

Geronimo Stilton

The Wonderful Wizard of Oz

Based on the novel
by L. Frank Baum

Scholastic Inc.

The Kansas Prairie

On the wide-open Kansas prairie, the FLAT GRAY land stretched on for miles in every direction, with fields as far as the eye could see. There were no signs, no trees, and no buildings — except for one small WOODEN farmhouse and its barn.

A young mouse named Dorothy lived in that house, along with her uncle Henry, who worked the farm, and her aunt Em, who handled the housework.

The farmhouse had only one room with a table, three chairs, a rusty old stove, a cupboard, two beds (one BiG and one small), and a trapdoor in the floor. The trapdoor led down to the storm cellar — a tiny underground room where the family could take shelter in case of a **tornado**. Tornados happen often in Kansas. They are powerful storms that can **destroy** everything in their path, even houses. **Squeak!**

Dorothy spent her days helping her aunt and uncle around the farm, **exploring** whenever she could, and playing with her loyal dog, Toto.

Aunt Em and Uncle Henry didn't have much time for *fun*. They loved Dorothy very much, but they also had to work **enormously** hard! They wanted to make the best life they could for their little family.

But Dorothy was a **lively** mouse, full of **JOY**. This was mostly thanks to Toto, who often caused mischief

and always made her laugh!

Most days on the farm were just like the last. But then, one day, something truly extraordinary happened . . .

The Great Tornado

That morning, a strange **WIND** was blowing. Uncle Henry noticed in the field to his right, the grass was **WAVING** to the left. In the field to his left, the grass was **WAVING** to the right. It seemed like the north wind and the south wind were both BLOWING hard against each other — and meeting in the exact spot where the farmhouse lay! HOLEY CHEESE!

Uncle Henry knew there was going to be a tornado. But it wasn't going to be just one tornado — it was going to be a terrifying double tornado!

Dorothy was playing in the field with Toto when she heard her uncle call her. She scooped up her dog in her arms and ran to him right away.

"Get inside and hold on to your tail!" Uncle Henry shouted, pushing her inside. "We have to go down to the cellar!"

He rushed across the room, opened the trapdoor, and led Aunt Em downstairs. Dorothy was about to follow when Toto escaped from her arms and ran to hide under the bed.

"Toto! This is no time for games!" Dorothy squeaked, scurrying after him.

Just then a deafening wind shook the walls and an enormouse GUST slammed against the farmhouse.

Dorothy lost her balance and tumbled to the floor! Chattering cheddar!

The powerful tornado hit the house with another violent burst of wind. This time, the wind pulled the house completely off the ground and lifted it into the air!

The house whirled around and around, rising quickly into the tornado's funnel. Before anyone could twitch a whisker, the tornado carried the house far away.

The wind wailed like an angry cat, and everything around Dorothy was **pitch dark**. How *FUR-RAISING*!

Toto raced from one side of the room to the other, terrified.

"Be careful, Toto!" Dorothy warned him, glancing at the open trapdoor in the middle of the floor.

The dog tried to back away, but he skidded too close to the trapdoor. A second later, he FELL through!

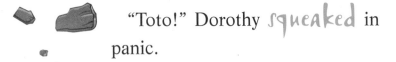

"Toto!" Dorothy *squeaked* in panic.

She inched closer to the trapdoor . . . and could hardly believe her eyes! The air pressure in the tornado funnel was holding Toto up! He hadn't tumbled far at all. Instead, he *floated on the wind*, just a few inches below the opening in the floor. Dorothy grabbed him by a paw, hoisted him up, and closed the trapdoor. What a *mousetastic* relief!

As the hours passed, Dorothy couldn't help getting her tail in a twist. Sooner or later, the **tornado** would calm down . . . and then what? *The house will crash to the ground!* she thought, her fur standing on end with fear.

But what could she do? She and Toto would just have to wait and see what happened. Exhausted, she STUMBLED to her bed and lay down.

Toto snuggled up next to her. Soon, despite the wailing wind, the two fell fast asleep. It had been an exhausting and exciting day — but their adventure was just beginning!

Four Strange Mice

A sudden, violent shake woke Dorothy with a START. She gasped and jumped to her paws. What had happened? The house seemed to have stopped moving, and dazzling sunshine filled the room with light.

Dorothy hurried to the door, with Toto hot on her paws. When she flung the door open, her eyes widened in wonder. Cheesy cream puffs — she was gazing out at a beautiful, COLORFUL landscape!

Dorothy was used to the flat gray Kansas prairie. She had never seen such fabumouse colors in her whole life!

There were GIGANTIC trees full of ripe fruit, a stream filled with fresh water, happily chirping birds with multicolored feathers, and bushes bursting with beautiful flowers . . .

Dorothy rubbed her eyes with her paws. Was she dreaming? Suddenly, she spotted four small figures walking toward her.

As they came closer, she saw that it was three small male mice and one small female mouse, not much taller than Dorothy herself. And they were dressed very strangely! All four wore cone-shaped hats, with tiny bells around the brim that jingled sweetly.

The female mouse was older than the others and had silver hair. She wore a

long white silk dress that sparkled in the SUNLIGHT.

The males were dressed in blue, and wore shiny boots that turned UP at the toe.

They stopped before they reached Dorothy, whispering and looking at her carefully.

Dorothy didn't move a whisker. Who could these strange rodents be?

The Munchkins

The mouse dressed in WHITE stepped toward Dorothy and bowed. "Welcome to the Land of the MUNCHKINS, most noble fairy," she squeaked in a lovely voice. "We are here to thank you for defeating the TERRIBLE Witch of the East, who was holding the Munchkins under her power."

Dorothy frowned. What Witch of the East?

"Um, actually," she said, "I'm not a fairy, I'm just a little mouselet. And I certainly haven't defeated anyone, especially not a witch . . ."

The mouse raised an eyebrow. "But your house fell ON TOP of her! Come see."

Dorothy followed the mouse around to the back of the farmhouse. Dorothy squeaked in shock! Two THIN legs with silver shoes on the paws were sticking out from under a corner of the house!

"Oh, cheese niblets!" she cried. "The farmhouse crushed her!"

"Don't worry, my dear," the mouse in white reassured her. "Those legs belong to an evil witch. Thanks to you, she can no longer harm the MUNCHKINS!"

Dorothy took a deep breath. Even though she was shaking in her fur, she couldn't help feeling curious. "Who are the Munchkins?"

"The rodents who live in this land," the mouse in white explained. "I'm the Witch of the North."

"Holey cheese!" Dorothy EXCLAIMED, twisting her whiskers. "Are you really a witch?"

The Witch of the North smiled sweetly. "Yes, dear, but I am a good witch, like the Witch of the South. Now that the Witch of the East has been defeated, only one bad witch remains in the kingdom of Oz: the WICKED Witch of the West. She is enormousely POWERFUL — much more powerful than me, I'm afraid!"

Dorothy stopped to think. "Oz? Is that what this place is called?"

The Witch of the North nodded. "Oz is the name of our land, as well as the great wizard of this world. He is more powerful than all of us witches put together. He lives in the Emerald City."

Just then the three Munchkin mice squeaked and pointed behind Dorothy.

Moldy mozzarella — the legs and paws of the witch under the house had vanished! Only the silver shoes remained. The Witch of the North gathered them up and handed them to Dorothy.

"She was so old that she dried up in the sun," she explained. "But these are enchanted shoes! You must take them."

Dorothy thanked the kind witch and took the shoes. They were truly fabumouse, but they frightened her a little. After all, they had just been on the paws of a TERRIFYING witch!

One, Two, Three!

Oz was marvemouse, but Dorothy couldn't help feeling homesick. She thought of Aunt Em and Uncle Henry, who were surely wondering where she was. A tear rolled down her snout. She sniffled. "I would like to return to my aunt and uncle's farm in Kansas right away. Can you help me?"

The other mice LOOKED confused.

"Kansas?" the first Munchkin repeated. "As far as I know, there's only desert to the East . . ."

"And it's the same to the South!" the second one said.

"The West is inhabited by the Winkies

and ruled by the WICKED WITCH OF THE WEST," the third added.

"The North is my country," continued the Witch of the North. "It is also bordered by the endless desert that surrounds Oz."

Dorothy twisted her tail in dismay. "Is there no way for me to go home?"

The Witch of the North took off her pointed hat, turned it over, and held the point in line with her snout. "One, two, three!" she cried.

Suddenly, the hat transformed into a blackboard! A message appeared, written in large chalk letters:

DOROTHY SHALL
GO TO THE
EMERALD CITY!

"Is your name Dorothy, by any chance?" the Witch of the North asked.

"Yes!" Dorothy replied, drying her eyes. She hadn't told them that! Maybe this place really was magical.

The Witch of the North smiled at her encouragingly. "Then you must go to the Emerald City! There you will find the Wizard of Oz. If anyone can help you, he can."

Dorothy's face LIT UP. "Where is this city?"

"It's in the middle of our kingdom," the Witch of the North explained. "It's a very long walk, across a countryside that is sometimes beautiful, and sometimes DANGEROUS. But don't worry — I will use every spell I know to protect you!"

With that, she bent down and gave

Dorothy a **kiss** on the forehead.

"There! No one would dare **harm** a mouse who has been kissed by the Witch of the North!"

There was a glimmering mark on Dorothy's face in the exact spot where the Witch had kissed her.

"The road to Emerald City is paved with yellow bricks the color of cheddar," the Witch added. "You can't miss it!"

With that, she turned three times on her left heel and DISAPPEARED. Then the three MUNCHKINS bowed and headed off into the woods. Cheese and crackers — Dorothy and Toto were really on their own now!

The Yellow Brick Road

There was no time to waste! Dorothy scurried around, gathering everything she needed for her trip to the Emerald City. But she was awfully hungry. The ripe fruit hanging on the trees around her made her mouth WATER. She couldn't resist picking a few pieces. Then she went back into the house, grabbed some slices of **BREAD** from the cupboard, and covered them with thick hunks of cheese. Yum — delicious!

She placed the bread in a basket. Then she put on her pink sunbonnet and looked down at her old leather shoes. Rats, they were so old and worn out!

This is going to be a long journey, she thought. I'll need shoes that are in good shape! I wonder if those beautiful silver shoes are the right size . . .

Dorothy tried on the silver shoes — and they fit perfectly! It was as though they had been made just for her paws.

Ready for an adventure, she picked up her basket, stepped outside, and closed the door behind her.

"Come on, Toto!" she said. "Let's go see the Wizard of Oz!"

The yellow brick road stretched out ahead like a river of cheese fondue!

Dorothy skipped along, Toto trotting joyfully in front of her. The sun shone high in the sky, the birds sang, and Dorothy felt hopeful. She was ready for an exciting adventure.

She had crashed right in the middle of an enchanted world, but she wasn't afraid. Everything here was so fabumouse — what could go wrong?

All Straw, No Brain!

After walking for a few miles, Dorothy stopped to rest. She leaned against the blue picket fence that lined the yellow brick road. Chattering cheddar — she really needed a break!

On the other side of the fence was an enormouse field of ripe golden corn. A scarecrow stood guard in the middle of the field.

Dorothy had seen many scarecrows in Kansas, so she knew that they kept crows OUT of the fields — but she had never seen one that looked so friendly!

She scurried over to get a better LOOK. Its head was made from a straw-stuffed

31

burlap sack with painted-on eyes, ears, nose, and mouth. It wore an old pointed hat like the ones the MUNCHKINS had worn. The rest of its body was made from worn-out, faded clothes stuffed with straw.

Just as Dorothy was admiring it, the Scarecrow winked at her.

Swiss cheese on rye, how strange!

Dorothy crept closer. Toto followed, barking and JUMPING up against the fence to get a better look.

The Scarecrow bowed his head politely.

"HELLO!" he greeted them. "How are you?"

"Fine, thank you," Dorothy replied slowly.

She wasn't too surprised that the Scarecrow was talking. After all, this was such an odd world, it seemed like anything could happen!

"I'm sad," the Scarecrow went on glumly.

"It's awfully boring to be **STUCK** up here all day!"

"Oh, you poor thing! Can't you get down?" Dorothy asked.

The Scarecrow shook his head. "I can't do it on my own. But if you could pull me down from this pole, I would be so grateful . . ."

Dorothy opened the gate in the fence and approached the Scarecrow. Then she quickly pulled him off the pole. He hardly weighed a thing!

Once he was down, the Scarecrow gave her a deep **bow** of gratitude. "You're so kind. Thank you! But who are you? And where are you headed?"

Dorothy grinned. "My name is Dorothy, and I'm going to the Emerald City to ask the Wizard of Oz to help me get home."

"Oz? Who is this wizard?" the Scarecrow replied, his eyes WIDENING.

She gasped. "Chewy cheddar! You don't know who he is?"

"Oh, I don't know anything about anything," the Scarecrow said with a shrug. "My head is full of STRAW, so I don't have any brains at all!"

Dorothy placed a paw on his shoulder. "Poor Scarecrow!"

"But listen," he confided, "maybe this wizard can give me a brain. I would really like to have one! I'm so tired of not knowing things . . ."

"Of course!" Dorothy smiled. "Come with us! I'm sure the Wizard of Oz will help you. I hope you're not afraid of a long journey."

"Oh, don't worry!" the Scarecrow assured her. "The only thing in the world I'm afraid of is FIRE. My straw would go up in flames before you could even twitch a whisker!"

With that, Dorothy and Toto continued along the yellow brick road with the Scarecrow alongside them. He even offered to carry Dorothy's basket. Thundering cattails, it was so nice to have found a friend!

Why Do You Want
to Go Home?

As they continued on their journey, the yellow brick road became more and more uneven. The bricks were full of **CRACKS** and holes!

Dorothy and Toto hopped along, being careful to avoid the roughest spots. But the Scarecrow kept stumbling. "Oh! Oh!" he gasped each time he fell, *waving* his straw-stuffed arms for help.

Every time, Dorothy ran to pick him up. Then he continued to trip merrily along, laughing at his own clumsiness. What a funny, *SILLY* friend he was turning out to be!

After a long walk, the trio stopped along the side of the road to have a snack. The Scarecrow was the only one who didn't eat. Since his stomach was full of STRAW, he never got hungry!

While they rested, Dorothy told him about Kansas and her life on the prairie.

"Why do you want to go back there?" the Scarecrow asked. "It sounds like Kansas is awfully flat and dull compared to the BEAUTY of Oz."

Dorothy sighed. "Oh, but Kansas is where my home and my family are! No place is more beautiful than your own home."

The Scarecrow shook his head and shrugged. "See, you can tell I don't have a brain! If I did, I would probably understand."

As they walked, the countryside around

them became **BARREN** and empty. When evening fell, the three friends found themselves at the edge of a vast forest.

Dorothy couldn't see much of anything, but the Scarecrow offered her his arm for support.

"I can see in the **DARK**!" he explained.

STUMBLING a bit, Dorothy and the Scarecrow entered the woods arm in arm, with Toto close behind.

"Look!" the Scarecrow said, pointing. "A cabin! Should we stop?"

"Oh, yes, I'm mousetastically tired!" Dorothy replied with a yawn.

The cabin was very tiny, and there was nothing inside but a bed of dried leaves.

Dorothy and Toto lay down and fell asleep immediately!

The Scarecrow, who was never tired, stood watch over his new friends and waited for Dawn. To pass the time, he examined a strange rusty can that had been abandoned in one corner. What could it be?

The Tin Woodman

Dorothy woke up to cheddar-colored sunbeams filtering gently through the cabin windows.

"I'm so thirsty!" she squeaked, stretching.

The Scarecrow shrugged helplessly. He had never been thirsty or hungry!

They walked to a nearby spring, where Dorothy and Toto drank some water and ate a bit of bread. As they munched on their breakfast, they heard a deep sigh.

Holey cheese, what was that?

They looked around but didn't see anything strange. But a few moments later, they heard the same voice moaning.

"Oh, ohhhh . . ."

Dorothy turned and noticed something sparkling in the sunlight. As she went for a closer look, her whiskers wobbled and her jaw dropped in surprise!

Next to the trunk of a LARGE felled tree, there was a woodman with his ax raised high in the air. But this was no ordinary woodman — he was made of tin! And it looked like he was stuck! His head, arms, and legs were welded to his body, and they all seemed very STIFF.

Toto started barking, but Dorothy and the Scarecrow bravely walked up to the tin woodman.

"Were you moaning?" asked Dorothy.

"Yes, that was me!" the Tin Woodman muttered through his tight jaw. A sob rumbled in his metal chest. "I've been

stuck here for over a year!"

"A year!" Dorothy replied, **shocked**. "Cheese niblets! How can we help you?"

The Woodman turned an **EYE** toward her, looking hopeful.

"In my cabin, there's an **OILCAN**. If you could use it to oil my joints, I would be so thankful!"

Dorothy *RUSHED* back to the cabin to get the oilcan that the Scarecrow had noticed the night before. In two shakes of a mouse's tail, she oiled all of the Woodman's joints from top to bottom.

Screek! Screeeech! Scrick!

Thundering cattails, the Tin Woodman made so much noise when he started to move! But soon he was as good as new.

He put his ax on the ground and smiled from ear to ear. "Thank you! You don't know how happy you've made me!"

Dorothy GRINNED. She loved being able to help people here in Oz!

Heart, Brain, and . . . Stomach!

The Tin Woodman asked his three new friends what they were doing in the woods.

"We're going to see the Wizard of Oz," Dorothy explained. "I'm hoping that he will help me and Toto get home to Kansas, and the Scarecrow wants to ask him for a brain."

The Woodman looked thoughtful. "Do you think the Wizard of Oz could give me a heart? I don't have one, but it's the thing I'd like most."

"Oh, I think so!" Dorothy declared. "If he can give the Scarecrow a brain, he could give you a heart. Come with us — it can't hurt to ask!"

The Tin Woodman rested the ax on his shoulder and asked Dorothy to keep the OILCAN in her basket. Then the friends continued along the yellow brick road.

At one point, the Scarecrow saw a BIG hole in front of him. As usual, he didn't do anything to avoid it — and as usual, he fell flat on his face! RATS!

"Why didn't you walk around the hole?" the Tin Woodman asked him, confused.

"I'm not smart enough to think of that!" the Scarecrow moaned. "That's why I'm asking the Wizard of Oz for a brain."

"I understand," the Woodman nodded sympathetically. "But you know, the brain isn't the most important thing. It's much, much more important to have a **heart**. The heart will always guide you to what's **good**."

The Scarecrow seemed like he was thinking — which was impossible, since he only had **STRAW** in his head!

"Well, you know what I say?" he finally declared. "I want a **brain**, because a fool wouldn't even know what to do with a heart."

"I still prefer the heart," the Woodman replied. "Because the brain can't make a person **happy**."

Dorothy had to admit, they both made good points!

But something else was **worrying** her — the **BREAD AND CHEESE** were almost gone, and all this walking was making her awfully *hungry*. She would give anything for a mozzarella milkshake!

The Scarecrow and Tin Woodman didn't need to **eat**, but she wasn't made of straw or tin. Dorothy wasn't thinking about her heart or her brain anymore — just her rumbling **stomach**!

A Cowardly Lion!

The yellow brick road wound through the forest, and Dorothy began to feel a little frightened. Holey cheese, there were shadows everywhere. Even the birds had stopped singing! How much longer did they have to go to get to the Emerald City?

Just as she was wondering this, a massive lion suddenly LEAPED out in front of them! **Holey cheese!** The enormouse cat struck the Scarecrow with one paw and knocked him to the ground, spilling STRAW everywhere. With another blow, he struck the Tin Woodman. He fell over with a mighty crash.

The Lion was just about to threaten Toto when Dorothy bravely stepped in front of him. As a mouse, she was a little scared of such a huge **CAT**. But she couldn't watch as the beastly **BULLY** picked on her friends.

"Hey!" she shouted. "You're so **BIG** and **strong** — why are you bothering creatures who are weaker than you? You might be a lion, but you sure are cowardly!"

She RUSHED to help the Scarecrow and the Tin Woodman back to their feet.

Ashamed, the Lion hung his shaggy head. "Everyone tells me I'm a big coward!" he admitted. "I don't know what to do about it. Anytime I have to fight someone my size or bigger, I start shaking in my fur!"

The Lion's paws trembled and tears rolled down his fur. "Whenever I come snout-to-snout with someone mighty, my heart **POUNDS**, my whiskers **wobble**, and I just want to run away!"

The Scarecrow and the Woodman stepped closer. Even Dorothy felt sorry for the Lion.

"Do you have a brain?" the Scarecrow asked nervously.

"I believe so," the Lion replied.

"And a heart?" the Tin Woodman asked. "Oh, but of course you do — you already said that it **POUNDS** when you're afraid!"

"You know," Dorothy said kindly, "we're going to see the Wizard of Oz to ask him for a brain, a heart, and help getting home."

The Lion blinked in surprise. "Oh! Do you think the Wizard of Oz would give me some **COURAGE**?"

Dorothy smiled. "Let's hope so. Come with us, and we'll find out!"

So the Lion joined the group on their journey. At first, Toto wasn't happy about this at all! He watched the Lion suspiciously and growled under his breath. But the Cowardly Lion was actually so sweet and gentle that before long, Toto started to think of him as a **friend**.

The Terrible Kalidahs

That NIGHT, the five travelers slept outside, under a leafy TREE.

The Tin Woodman lit a small FIRE — and the Scarecrow stayed far away! He gathered nuts for Dorothy. The bread in the basket was almost gone, and he knew that she would need something to eat.

Dorothy was lucky to have found such kind and thoughtful new friends!

The NIGHT passed peacefully, but none of them realized that the next day would be full of adventure!

At Dawn, they continued along the yellow brick road. Before long, they came upon a deep ditch. The ditch split the entire forest in two! The banks were steep and covered in SHARP rocks.

"What now?" Dorothy asked with a sigh.

The Scarecrow extended one of his straw arms. "We can't fly, that's for sure. We can't climb or JUMP over it. So the only thing to do is to stop where we are."

"Well . . ." the Cowardly Lion began quietly, "I *could* jump over it. And maybe, if I take you one at a time, we could ALL jump across!"

"I'll go first!" the Scarecrow offered. "If we fall, it won't hurt me."

The others smiled. Sometimes it seemed as though the Scarecrow already had a brain!

Trembling with fear, the Lion hoisted the Scarecrow onto his back, stepped up to the edge of the ditch, and took a mighty LEAP.

Rancid ricotta, Dorothy couldn't watch! She covered her eyes with her paws.

And then — **hooray**! The Lion and the Scarecrow made it safely to the other side.

"Good job, Lion!" Dorothy cheered, jumping for JOY.

One by one, the Lion carried the others across the ditch. On the opposite side, the forest seemed even darker. No sunlight filtered through the leaves, and strange HOWLS echoed everywhere.

"The **KALIDAHS**!" the Cowardly Lion gasped, twisting his tail.

Dorothy gulped. "Wh-wh-who are the Kalidahs?"

"Monstrous beasts, with the body of a bear and the head of a tiger!" the Lion whispered, covering his snout with his paws. "Their CLAWS are so sharp that they could slice me in two with one swipe!"

But the Lion didn't have time to say anything more, because they had reached the edge of a CLiFF. Once again, they needed to come up with a plan — and FAST!

This time, the Scarecrow came up with an idea. "Woodman, this is your moment!" he cried. "You can cut down that big TREE over there with your ax and make it fall so that it creates a **BRIDGE**. Then getting to the other side will be **easy cheesy**!"

The others looked at him, more surprised than ever. The Scarecrow was full of **fabumouse** ideas!

The Woodman agreed, and **chopped** down a tree at the edge of the **RAVINE**. It fell across the gap, creating the perfect bridge. Then the Scarecrow, Dorothy, Toto, the Cowardly Lion, and the Tin Woodman carefully headed across the tree trunk.

They were about halfway across when a loud **HOWL** made them jump and look behind them.

"What did I tell you? It's the **KALIDAHS**!" cried the Lion in panic.

A pack of terrible Kalidahs burst out of the forest and headed straight for the TREE TRUNK. Crusty cat litter, they were coming after Dorothy and her friends!

Dorothy tried not to panic, but it was no use. The Kalidahs were so close! She covered her face with her paws in despair.

"Ohhh! **WE'RE DONE FOR!**" she cried.

River Rafting

The Kalidahs moved toward Dorothy and her friends. Their jaws were wide open and DRIPPING with slobber.

"Stay calm!" cried the Scarecrow. "If the Woodman chops the trunk as soon as we reach the other side, the Kalidahs will all fall into the RAVINE!"

Without a moment to waste, the five friends scurried along, trying hard to keep their balance.

When they finally reached the other side of the ravine, the Tin Woodman quickly brandished his ax and chopped through the tree trunk.

The Kalidahs gripped the bark with their

SHARP claws, but finally slipped and tumbled into the depths below.

THUNDERING CATTAILS! Dorothy and her brave friends had escaped DANGER by a whisker!

Here the forest was bright again, and the trees and bushes weren't as thick.

"Look!" the Woodman cried, pointing into the distance. "There's a river!"

He was right — a large river flowed peacefully nearby. On the other side of the river was the yellow brick road!

"How can we get across?" Dorothy asked, peering around.

Once again, it was the Scarecrow who had the solution!

He asked the Tin Woodman to cut down more tree trunks. Then they could make a RAFT that would take them to the other side!

Before they knew it, the friends found themselves floating on a raft down the river, paddling with LONG poles. They were about halfway across when a strong current pushed the raft off course.

"Oh no!" Dorothy squeaked. "**RATS!** Now we'll never get to the other side!"

"What a mess!" the Woodman cried. "This river flows right to the Land of the **WICKED WITCH OF THE WEST**!"

The Scarecrow tried to stop the raft by **sticking** his pole into the river bottom. But his body was too light to hold the raft back. The raft kept moving — while the Scarecrow and his pole stayed **STUCK**!

"Farewell, **friends**!" the poor STRAW man called sadly.

"No!" squeaked Dorothy.

The Tin Woodman started to cry, but then

remembered that it would just make his face **rusty**. So he quickly dried his tears.

They had to do something. They couldn't *abandon* their friend!

Have Courage!

As the current carried the raft AWAY, the Cowardly Lion shook his mane with determination.

"Have courage!" he cried. "We can do this!"

The friends looked around, trying to come up with a plan — FAST!

"Grab my tail and hold on," the Lion instructed Dorothy, the Tin Woodman, and Toto. "I'll swim and tow the RAFT to shore!"

It took a long time and amazing amounts of strength, but at last the **powerful** Lion managed to pull all his friends to safety . . . except one!

The Scarecrow was still stuck in the

middle of the river, looking more discouraged than ever.

Dorothy and the others stared at him hopelessly from the riverbank. Holey cheese, what could they do?

Just then an enormouse stork landed a few steps away from them.

"Hello there!" she said pleasantly. "What are you doing in these parts?"

"We're on our way to see the Wizard of Oz," Dorothy squeaked sadly.

"Oh, but this isn't the right way!" the Stork objected.

"Yes, we know," Dorothy nodded. "But do you see that Scarecrow over there? He's one of our friends, and he's STUCK in the middle of the river. We can't go to the Emerald City without him!"

The Stork looked at the Scarecrow, then

back at Dorothy, thinking hard.

"Maybe I could try to carry him," she suggested. "As long as he's not too **HEAVY** . . ."

"Oh, he's VERY LIGHT!" Dorothy beamed. "He's made of STRAW!"

The Stork flew into the air, grabbed the Scarecrow by his shirt, and managed to **CARRY** him to the riverbank faster than a mouse on a cheese hunt.

The Scarecrow was so **happy** to be back with his friends that he hugged them all and danced with JOY.

Dorothy smiled at the Stork gratefully. "I don't know what we would have done without your help!"

"Oh, it was nothing!" the Stork said, **blushing**. "Now I must go, because

my little ones are waiting for me in our nest. Safe travels! And good luck!"

"Thanks again!" the friends all shouted as the Stork took off into the sky.

The Enchanted Poppies

Before long, Dorothy and her friends came across an **enormouse** field of fragrant **scarlet** poppies. The flowers were enchanted! Their scent was so strong that anyone who breathed it in would fall fast asleep. And if the sleepers weren't taken far away from the flowers, they would sleep forever!

Since Dorothy didn't know this, she sniffed the poppies many times — they smelled fabumouse! In no time, she began to feel her eyelids grow **HEAVY**, until she and Toto both fell into a deep sleep.

"Now what?" asked the Tin Woodman.

"If we leave her here, I'm afraid she'll sleep forever," replied the Lion. "I'm having a hard time keeping my eyes OPEN, and Toto is already asleep."

The Woodman and the Scarecrow couldn't smell anything, though, so they were wide awake.

The Scarecrow immediately recognized the DANGER and told the Lion, "You must get far away from here, or you'll fall asleep, too! We'll take care of Dorothy and Toto — now go!"

TERRIFIED, the lion leaped to his paws and fled.

The Woodman took Dorothy in his arms, the Scarecrow picked up Toto, and they continued on their journey. Step by step, they followed the yellow brick road through the poppy field, until they glimpsed a **HUGE** figure lying in the flowers. It was the Cowardly Lion! The smell of the poppies had overwhelmed him, and now he was fast asleep.

"He's too **HEAVY** for us," the Tin Woodman moaned. "We'll have to leave him here!"

Looking sadly back over their shoulders, they walked on, leaving the poor Lion behind.

Some Helping Paws

The Scarecrow and Tin Woodman continued walking with Dorothy and Toto in their arms. It seemed like the field of poppies would never end! But finally they reached a clearing without flowers, at the edge of a river.

They lay Dorothy and Toto on the ground and fanned some *AIR* over them to chase away the poisonous poppy scent.

The Scarecrow sighed. "Let's hope we find the yellow brick ro —"

A deafening meow echoed in the clearing, making the two friends jump.

Thundering cattails, what was that?

Before they knew it, a strange animal leaped out of the grass. It was an enormouse **WILD CAT** with dark **FUR**! It had bright yellow eyes and tremendous jaws with two rows of **SHARP**, glistening teeth.

It was truly terrifying! And it was quickly moving toward them!

The Woodman realized that the cat was following a little gray rabbit. Even though he didn't have a **heart**, he couldn't let the beast do something terrible to the innocent bunny. Without hesitating, he raised his ax. It came down right in front of the cat, who nearly jumped out of his fur and ran away as fast as his paws would take him!

The Rabbit huffed and puffed, trying

to catch her breath. "Puff, puff . . .
Thank you! Pant, pant . . . You saved
my life!"

"Oh, it was nothing," the Woodman said,
kicking the dirt. "I don't have a heart, you
know, but I always try to help out anyone in
trouble — even a simple rabbit!"

"What do you mean, 'simple rabbit'?!" the
Rabbit replied, annoyed. "I am a queen!
The Queen of the Rabbits."

"Oh, I beg your pardon!" the Woodman
cried. He gave a deep bow, which made him
squeak and creak all over.

Just then a band of rabbits hopped up and
surrounded the Queen.

"This FUNNY man of tin saved me,"
she declared. "In exchange, you will do
anything that he wishes!"

The Rabbits nodded enthusiastically.

"What can we do for you, sir?"

The Woodman shrugged his shoulders, unsure of what to say. But the Scarecrow said, "We need you to help transport our friend the Lion, who fell asleep in the poppy field! Can you find some ropes?"

The Rabbits sprang into action, rushing off to find ropes.

"And you, Woodman," the Scarecrow continued, "use your ax to cut down some trees and build a WOODEN cart!"

While Dorothy and Toto continued to sleep peacefully, their friends built a large cart, using four thick slices of tree trunks for wheels.

The Rabbits found some rope and tied it to the front of the cart.

PULLING all together, with the help of the Woodman and the Scarecrow, the

Rabbits managed to drag the cart all the way to the Cowardly Lion. They piled the huge creature on top and pulled him to the clearing safe and sound. **HOLEY CHEESE** — what a feat!

A Green House
Fit for a Mouse

When Dorothy, Toto, and the Cowardly Lion awoke, the Rabbits were staring at them, curious and a little afraid.

As soon as Dorothy learned what had happened, she thanked them all for their help.

The Queen of the Rabbits said good-bye and gave Dorothy a tiny silver whistle. "If you ever need our help again, use this WHISTLE," she said. "We'll come to your aid!"

Then she and the rest of the Rabbits hopped away.

"Crusty cat litter! I may be **BIG** and

fearsome, but some simple flowers poisoned me, and some little rabbits saved my life!" the Cowardly Lion said. "You just never know what will happen."

Relieved to be out of DANGER, the five friends continued along and soon spotted the familiar yellow brick road. Here, the road was smooth and lined with a picket fence, just like it had been at the beginning of their journey. The only difference was that now the picket fence was green instead of blue.

On each side of the path were fields as green as **emeralds**. Soon, small green

houses came into view, with little mice peeking out of them. The mice looked a bit like the MUNCHKINS, but they wore emerald-green clothes and pointed hats. And for some reason,

they didn't seem to be very friendly.

Summoning their **courage**, the five friends walked up to one of the houses. Dorothy knocked on the front door.

KNOCK, KNOCK!

A rodent cracked the door open and eyed them suspiciously.

"What do you want?" she asked.

Dorothy noticed right away that the rodent was peering at the Lion. She rushed to reassure the mouse.

"Oh, don't be afraid — my friend would never hurt anyone!"

The mouse paused for a moment, then asked, "Where are you headed?"

"To the Emerald City!" replied Dorothy. "We're going to see the great Wizard of Oz."

The rodent raised an eyebrow. "No one

has **EVER** seen the great Oz!"

Dorothy and her friends looked at one another in dismay.

"But how can that be?" the Scarecrow asked.

"He always stays in the palace throne room," the mouse explained. "Even his employees have never seen his true face! He's so powerful that he can take on any APPEARANCE he wishes. To some, he appears as an elephant, to others, a tiger, a fairy, or an elf. I assure you, there's no one in the world who can say for sure what the Wizard of Oz looks like."

Dorothy sighed. "But we need his help. We've traveled SO FAR!"

"What is it you need?" the rodent asked, curious.

"I must get back **home** to Kansas,

the Scarecrow would like a **brain**, the Tin Woodman wishes for a **heart**, and the Cowardly Lion wants **courage**," Dorothy explained, chewing on her pawnails nervously.

"Don't worry," the mouse assured her. "I don't know where Kansas is, but Oz knows every place in existence. And he has a ton of brains, **hearts** of every size, and an **enormouse** jar stuffed with courage! If you manage to get in to see him, I know he will be able to help with **ALL** your requests."

The Guardian
of the City

The kind mouse offered to let Dorothy and her friends stay for the NIGHT. She gave them dinner and settled Dorothy and Toto in a comfortable room, while the Lion curled up outside the door. The Scarecrow and the Tin Woodman didn't eat or sleep, because they didn't need to, but they enjoyed taking a break.

The following day, refreshed and full of energy, the five friends continued on their journey to the Emerald City.

They walked all morning and afternoon, until they reached a TREMENDOUSLY tall gate. It was covered in sparkling emeralds.

There was a bell right next to
the MAJESTIC gate. Dorothy
rang it, and the doors swung open
immediately.

The five friends stepped over the
threshold and found themselves in a room
where the walls shimmered with emeralds.
The Guardian of the City stood stiffly in the
center of the room. He was a small mouse
no taller than a **MUNCHKIN**, dressed
all in green. An enormouse green trunk
stood next to him.

"What do you want?" the mouse
asked sharply.

"We've come to see the Wizard of Oz,"
Dorothy replied.

The mouse JUMPED back. "Oz?! But
it's been years and years since anyone has
asked to see him!"

Dorothy wasn't about to give up. "Please, sir, let us pass. It's very important!"

The Guardian scratched his snout, unsure.

"If it's truly important, I will let you pass. But you must understand: If you want to see the Wizard only out of curiosity, or if you plan to bother him with some kind of foolishness, you'll be locked up!"

Dorothy shivered. Moldy mozzarella, the Wizard sounded awfully MEAN!

The Emerald City

The Guardian of the Emerald City studied Dorothy and her friends carefully.

"Oz is a very good and just wizard," he explained. "But when someone bothers him, he has been known to get ANGRY!"

The Scarecrow took a step forward. "We don't want to bother him," he said. "But we've made a long journey to get here. We have some very serious requests."

"In that case," the Guardian squeaked with a smile, "come here and put on these glasses."

He opened the green trunk. It was full of glasses of every shape and size. All of

them had green lenses.

The five friends carefully approached the trunk.

"Why do we need to wear glasses?" Dorothy asked, confused. "I can see just fine!"

"Oh, everyone must put on glasses before they enter the Emerald City," the Guardian explained. "Otherwise, its shiny splendor will blind you. Even the rodents who live in the city wear them DAY and NIGHT!"

Dorothy and her friends each picked out a pair of glasses. Even Toto found a **tiny** pair! The Guardian adjusted his own glasses on his snout, grabbed a large golden key hanging from a hook on the wall, and opened the door that led into the marvemouse Emerald City.

HOLEY CHEESE!

The beautiful city made Dorothy squeak with joy. The sparkling green light was so **intense** that, even with the glasses, it took a little while for their eyes to adjust.

The streets and buildings were all made of emerald-green marble, and rows and rows of emeralds shone everywhere. The roads were crowded with rodents all dressed in green. The stores and everything sold in them were **GREEN**, too, including the food and drinks!

The mice bustling around seemed very busy, but they also looked mousetastically **happy**.

Dorothy didn't have too much time to look around. Instead, her attention was quickly

drawn to the MAJESTIC palace of the Wizard of Oz. It rose powerfully from the heart of the city.

Moldy mozzarella — after a long, DANGEROUS adventure, they were finally almost there!

Inside Oz's Palace

A bearded mouse in uniform guarded the entrance to the palace of Oz.

The Guardian of the Emerald City stepped forward and cleared his throat. "These strangers wish to see the **GREAT** Oz!" he announced.

The guard agreed to let them pass, and they headed through the doors of the grand palace. Dorothy's tail trembled with excitement!

Squeakless, the five friends made their way into an enormouse green hall, sparkling with emeralds as far as the eye could see. Swiss cheese on rye, it was beautiful!

The guard asked Dorothy and her friends

to wipe their paws on a green **STRAW MAT**, then to make themselves at home.

"Just wait here," he said **kindly**. "I'll go to the throne room and announce your visit to the great Wizard."

They waited for what seemed like hours! Just when Dorothy was about to lose hope, the guard reappeared.

"It was more difficult than I expected," he explained. "The Wizard had no desire to see you. But when I said that you were wearing a pair of silver shoes, and that you had a strange **mark** on your forehead, he suddenly agreed. However, he said you must each appear before him one at a time, on **different** days."

The five friends looked at each other and shrugged. What could they do?

The guard continued, "Obviously, you

will be guests here at the palace for several **DAYS**."

They would get to stay in this fabumouse place! Dorothy could hardly believe it.

But the surprises weren't over. Soon, a *charming* mouse appeared, dressed in green from head to tail, and led Dorothy to the room where she and Toto would be staying.

It was marvemouse! There was a **warm**, **soft** bed, a tiny fountain that bubbled in a marble basin, windows adorned with flowers, shelves with books full of funny illustrations, and a wardrobe stuffed with clothes, all Dorothy's size. And everything — absolutely everything — was **GREEN**!

All of Dorothy's friends were led to their rooms, too, and each one got busy settling into his comfortable quarters.

Dorothy and Toto slept **peacefully**.

The Scarecrow, on the other paw, couldn't get used to his **FANCY** room and soft bed. He didn't lie down at all! Instead, he just stood next to the bed, straight as a board, and waited for **Dawn**. Rancid ricotta, what a long night!

The Tin Woodman didn't need to close his **EYES**, either, but he tried to lie down anyway and enjoy his comfortable room. But instead he spent the **NIGHT** moving his joints one by one, to keep them from getting stuck or **rusting**.

The Cowardly Lion would have preferred to lie down in a nice bed of **soft** grass rather than the fancy **CANOPY** bed he found in his room. But he didn't want to be rude, so he curled up carefully on the mattress and fell into a deep sleep.

And so the five friends spent a peaceful night in the palace of Oz. They had no idea what surprises the next DAY would bring, but they wanted to be ready!

The Great Wizard of Oz

The next morning, Dorothy put on a GREEN dress and a beautiful green pinafore. Toto even had a green ribbon tied around his neck! Then a kind mouse led them to the throne room entrance.

Dorothy's fur STOOD ON END. She had heard so many different things about the Wizard of Oz that she didn't know what to expect!

Outside the throne room, many rodents were milling around, all dressed in elaborate, fabumouse clothing.

"They come here every day," the kind

mouse explained to Dorothy. "But only because they have nothing else to do. None of them have ever been admitted to see the **great Oz**!"

Suddenly, a *bell* echoed through the hall. A mouse quickly motioned Dorothy to step forward. "That's the signal! Oz is waiting for you."

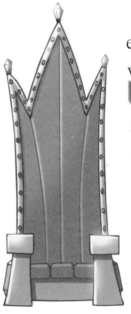

Shaking in her fur, Dorothy entered the throne room and was immediately struck by a **blinding** light. Thousands of shining green emeralds reflected all around her — from the walls, the floor, and even the ceiling!

Dorothy noticed a small screen off in one corner, but she could hardly take her eyes off the enormouse, MAJESTIC marble throne in the center of the room.

HOLEY CHEESE!

There was no one actually sitting on the throne. Not an elephant, not a fairy, not an elf — none of the creatures Dorothy had heard about. There was only a **HUGE HEAD** hovering over the seat, with eyes, nose, and a mouth bigger than a **giant's**!

Squeak! Dorothy turned as white as a slab of mozzarella cheese!

The Wizard's two immense eyes fell on her. Then he spoke in a **thundering** voice. "I am the great and terrible Oz. Who are you? And why have you come to see me?"

"I am Dorothy," she squeaked quietly. "I'm here to ask for your help!"

The huge eyes studied her closely. "Why are you wearing those **shoes**?"

Dorothy twisted her tail and replied, "They are the silver shoes of the **EVIL** Witch of the East. My house fell on her during a **tornado**, and the Witch of the North told me that I should take them."

"And why do you have that **mark** on your forehead?" the Wizard asked.

"That's where the Witch of the North **kissed** me before sending me here," Dorothy explained. "I just want to go home to Kansas — can you help me?"

"Why should I help you?" the Wizard asked.

Dorothy looked down at the ground. "Because you are a **great** and **powerful** wizard, and I am just a poor, **helpless** mouse."

"You have defeated the Witch of the East," the Wizard boomed. "So you must be able to defeat the Witch of the West, too. Do that, and I will help you return to Kansas!"

Dorothy **STARED** at him in disbelief. "But I didn't defeat anyone — it was an accident! I could never hurt anybody, not even a WICKED witch!"

"That doesn't matter to me," Oz pronounced. "If you do not defeat the WICKED Witch of the West, you will **neveR** return home!"

The Many
Faces of Oz

Dorothy left the throne room with her tail between her legs.

Outside, her friends were waiting anxiously for her.

"Well? How did it go?" they asked.

"Oh, I'll never be able to go home!" she squeaked, TEARS rolling down her snout. "Oz wants me to defeat the WICKED Witch of the West before he'll help me!"

Her friends tried to comfort her, but they knew that none of them could change the Wizard's mind.

Dorothy spent the rest of the day in her room trying to think of a solution without

much luck. After a long, exhausting day, she finally fell asleep.

The next morning, it was the Scarecrow's turn to see the Wizard. When he entered the throne room, he found himself in front of the most beautiful creature he had ever encountered — a fairy! Emerald-green curls tumbled onto her shoulders, and two green wings fluttered on her back. She wore a green silk dress and a sparkling emerald tiara.

"I am the great and TERRIBLE Oz," she declared in a sweet voice that contradicted what she was saying. "Who are you? And why have you come to see me?"

Trembling, the Scarecrow bowed clumsily. (With all that stuffing, it wasn't easy to bow!)

"I — I am just a simple Scarecrow, stuffed with **STRAW**," he said quickly. "I'm here because I really want a brain."

"I do not grant favors without asking for something in return," the fairy replied. "If you want a **brain**, you must defeat the **WICKED** Witch of the West!"

The Scarecrow returned to his **friends**, heartbroken, and told them about his meeting with the fairy.

The same thing happened the next day, when the Tin Woodman had his turn in front of the Wizard. This time, the Wizard took the form of a terrible, ferocious **BEAST**! He was as **BIG** as an elephant and had a head like a rhinoceros, but with five eyes!

Luckily, the Tin Woodman didn't have a heart, so he couldn't be truly afraid.

"I am the great and terrible Oz," the beast

roared. "Who are you? Why have you come to see me?"

"I am the Tin Woodman, and I'm here to ask you for a **heart**," the Woodman replied. "I want to love again!"

"If you wish for a heart," the beast replied, "you must earn it. Defeat the Witch of the West, and you will have the kindest heart in the kingdom!"

The poor Woodman returned to his friends, miserable.

Finally, it was the Lion's turn. When he arrived in the throne room, the great Oz transformed into an enormouse, flaming ball of **FIRE**!

But when the fireball spoke, its voice was very calm. "I am the great and terrible Oz. Who are you? And why have you come to see me?"

The Lion tried to step closer, but SCORCHED his whiskers. Rotten rat's teeth! "I am a Cowardly Lion," he replied, rubbing his singed snout. "I'm here because I would like some courage so I can finally become a worthy king of beasts!"

The fireball flared up, then gave a familiar reply. "Defeat the WICKED Witch of the West, and you will have all the courage and confidence that you desire!"

The Lion bowed his head and left the room, **disheartened**.

For the love of cheese, what were they going to do?

We Won't Leave You Alone!

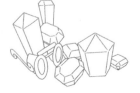The five friends stood outside the throne room for a while, discouraged.

"We must go to the Land of the **Winkies** and defeat the **WICKED** Witch of the West!" the Lion suddenly roared. "We can't give up on our wishes now!"

"But how in the name of all things cheesy can we defeat a wicked witch? And what if we fail?" Dorothy squeaked.

"Then I will still be the most cowardly lion in history," the Lion declared glumly.

"And I will never love anyone again!" the Tin Woodman said, beating his empty tin chest.

"As for me," the Scarecrow added, "bye-bye, brain!"

Dorothy dried her TEARS and started thinking. Her friends were right. They couldn't give up on their dreams now!

"Toto and I will go find the Witch of the West," she declared, smoothing her fur. "I have no idea how to defeat a witch, but we'll come up with something. Right, Toto?"

The dog raised his eyes and looked worried.

"You're going **alone**? Never!" the Cowardly Lion said. "I'll come with you. Even though I'm too cowardly to face a WITCH, maybe I can still be helpful!"

"Do you think I'm going to stay here twiddling my thumbs, waiting for you?"

the Scarecrow asked, waving his long straw arms around. "No way — I'm coming, too! Even if I don't have any ideas in this head of mine, I'll help you however I can."

The Tin Woodman smiled. "What about me? I couldn't hurt a fly, let alone a WITCH! But I won't let you go without me."

So it was decided — the five friends were off on a **dangerous** adventure to the Land of the Winkies!

None of them could defeat the Witch alone. But cheesy cream puffs — maybe they would be able to do it together! They'd gotten this far, hadn't they?

With some pep in their paws, all five friends drifted off to sleep. They had a **long, long** day ahead of them!

Marching West

The next morning, Dorothy and her friends got ready to depart.

The Woodman sharpened his ax and had the Lion oil his joints. The Scarecrow stuffed himself with fresh STRAW, and Dorothy touched up the paint on his eyes so that he could see better. Dorothy refilled her little basket with food and tied a new green ribbon around Toto's neck. They were ready to start their new journey!

The guard with the long BEARD led them back to the Emerald City gates. There, the Guardian let them take off their green-lensed glasses.

"Pardon me, sir," Dorothy asked the

Guardian. "Which way should we go to find the WITCH OF THE WEST?"

"What a silly question!" the Guardian replied. "West, of course. Head for the place where the SUN sets!"

Waving good-bye, the five nervous **friends** walked west.

Dorothy was wearing the green silk dress she had put on for her meeting with Oz, but now it inexplicably turned as WHITE as SNOW! The same thing happened to the ribbon around Toto's neck. How strange!

As Dorothy and her friends walked, the land became more **rugged** and mountainous. There were no houses or farms, just land. The sun beat down on them. At last, the exhausted group stopped to rest.

Meanwhile, someone else was watching

them, too, but from afar! The WICKED Witch of the West only had one eye, but it was as powerful as a telescope.

That afternoon, standing at the lookout in front of her castle, she noticed this group of intruders pass through the borders of her land. The wicked Witch of the West immediately gave a blast on a silver WHISTLE. Suddenly, a **fierce** pack of wolves appeared out of nowhere.

"Get rid of those strangers!" she ordered. The wolves raced off to **attack**.

Luckily, the Scarecrow and the Woodman were WIDE AWAKE! As soon as they spotted the wolf pack approaching, they got ready to defend their friends.

"I can handle this battle," the Woodman

said to the TERRIFIED Scarecrow, taking up his ax. "Let me chase them off!"

Since he didn't have a heart, the Woodman was not afraid! He fearlessly THREW himself right into the middle of the wolf pack. Without hesitating, he swung and chopped with his GREAT ax. Before long, the BEASTS ran far away, frightened and howling.

Dorothy, Toto, and the Lion didn't notice a thing — they kept right on sleeping! Holey cheese, they were exhausted. But when they woke up and heard what had happened, they couldn't believe their ears — they were lucky to have such a brave friend!

Attacks!

As soon as the WITCH OF THE WEST saw her ferocious wolves yelping and racing back to her, she was FURIOUS. She grabbed her silver whistle again, and this time she blew on it twice.

The second WHISTLE was still ringing in the air when a flock of black crows crowded the entrance to the Witch's castle, **blocking** out the sky.

"Those strangers have dared to defy me!" the Witch screeched. "Crows, *get rid of them*!"

The flock of black birds rose into the sky, then DOVE toward Dorothy and her friends.

This time, it was the Scarecrow who stepped forward. "I know ALL about crows! I do nothing but chase them off from morning until night! Leave this to me."

His friends flattened themselves on the ground while the Scarecrow remained standing. He straightened up as tall as he could, and raised his head high.

Forty crows flew straight at the HEROIC Scarecrow, but he managed to ward them off, flinging the birds away one after another. He seemed unstoppable!

When the Witch of the West checked in again, she received a bitter surprise! All her loyal crows were lying on the ground, exhausted. Meanwhile, the five strangers trotted merrily on their way.

The Witch began to shake with anger. "It cannot be!" she shouted. "Now I will show you what a real WITCH can do!"

With that, she blew three times on her WHISTLE. A swarm of black bees swirled obediently around her.

"Sting them!" the Witch howled. "Sting them all!"

But when he heard the bees coming, the Scarecrow had another brilliant idea.

"Woodman!" he cried. "Take out all my straw and cover up Dorothy, Toto, and the Cowardly Lion. You'll be safe, because the bees cannot sting METAL. When they attack you, all their stingers will break against the tin. Then they won't be able to hurt anyone!"

The Woodman hurried to pull all the straw out of his friend's body. Soon the Scarecrow was sagging on the ground.

Meanwhile, the faithful Lion gathered

Dorothy and Toto in his paws and curled up with them on the ground. The Woodman covered all three of them with the Scarecrow's **STRAW**.

The swarm of bees flung themselves **ferociously** at the poor Woodman. But as soon as they tried to sting him, they **clanked** against the metal. Good-bye, stingers!

The bees quickly buzzed back to the **CASTLE**, battered and bruised.

Once they'd disappeared, Dorothy, the Lion, and the Woodman hurried to re-stuff the Scarecrow with straw. He looked even better than before!

The **WITCH** of the West was so furious that she stomped her paws, **TUGGED** at her fur, gnashed her yellow teeth, waved her ratty umbrella, and then sent for twelve

YELLOW-FURRED Winkies, her trusted servants.

"I've had **enough**!" she squeaked. "Capture the intruders! Do whatever you have to do to get rid of them once and for all!"

The **Winkies** weren't brave at all, but they couldn't disobey the WICKED WITCH. Resigned, they headed for the group of strangers. But when they saw the Cowardly Lion, the poor Winkies were so afraid that they ran off like mice on a cheese hunt!

The WITCH of the West was outraged. How could five strangers manage to escape her powerful attacks over and over again? Nothing like this had ever happened before!

She had no choice now but to use her GOLDEN CAP. This wasn't just any

hat! It was enchanted. Whoever wore it could call for help from the Flying Monkeys three times. The monkeys would carry out any command — but only three times!

The Witch had already been in trouble twice before and had needed to rely on her Golden Cap.

The first time was when she had enslaved all the Winkies and proclaimed herself their QUEEN. The second time, she had declared WAR on the great Oz himself and had chased him out of the West.

Now she could call on the powers of the Golden Cap only one more time — and she knew that this was exactly the right moment!

Ziz-zy, Zuz-zy, Zik!

The wicked Witch placed the Golden Cap on her head, balanced on her left paw, and carefully squeaked the magic spell: "Ep-pe, pep-pe, kak-ke!" She switched to her right paw and raised her voice: "Hil-lo, hol-lo, hel-lo!" Then she placed both paws on the ground and boomed, "Ziz-zy, zuz-zy, zik!"

The sky darkened. When the sun emerged, a swarm of shrieking **Flying Monkeys** had appeared!

The largest monkey, the **chief**, approached the Witch. "This is the third time that you have called on us for help. What is your command?"

The Witch did not hesitate. "**Get rid** of those intruders immediately! But bring the Lion to me — I want to put him to work."

The chief nodded, and the swarm of Monkeys zipped into the air and **DOVE** toward Dorothy and her **friends**.

Unfortunately, it all happened so quickly that the group was completely UNPREPARED! The Flying Monkeys grabbed the Tin Woodman and threw him against some **ROCKS**. Dented and bruised, the poor Woodman couldn't get up off the ground.

Then the Monkeys went after the Scarecrow, tearing into him with their **SHARP** claws and pulling out his **STRAW**. Then they gathered his head, hat, boots, and clothes and tossed them into a tall **TREE**.

Meanwhile, some of the Monkeys had seized the Lion. They tied him with a big

rope and heaved him up over their shoulders. Beating their huge wings, they carried him off to the Witch's **CASTLE**.

But the Monkeys didn't harm Dorothy. The chief noticed the mark on her forehead. He knew exactly what it meant!

"We cannot **attack** this mouselet," he declared. "She has been **kissed** by the Witch of the North! All we can do is take her to the Witch of the West's **CASTLE**."

The Flying Monkeys **gently** lifted Dorothy (with Toto in her arms), flew her to the castle, and left her on the doorstep. Then they **DISAPPEARED**.

In the Clutches of the Witch of the West

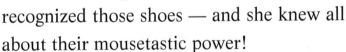

The Witch of the West was furious when she saw the mark on Dorothy's forehead. Rat-munching rattlesnakes — the mouselet was protected by the forces of GOOD! But when the Witch saw the silver shoes on Dorothy's paws, she began shaking in her fur. She recognized those shoes — and she knew all about their mousetastic power!

She was about to run from Dorothy as fast as her paws would take her, but then she paused. If Dorothy hadn't used the shoes to save herself yet, maybe she didn't realize

how powerful they were . . .

"I have decided not to HARM you," she said slowly, "but you must obey my every command — otherwise I will not be so kind to your dog, or your lion friend. From now on, you will be my loyal servant!"

The Witch led her to the CASTLE kitchen. "Wash the dishes, sweep the floor, and tend the FIRE," she commanded.

Without a single squeak, Dorothy immediately began cleaning.

Then the Witch went to the Lion's cage, determined to dress him up as a horse and put him to work. "I will be the only witch in the land with a carriage drawn by a lion!" she cackled.

But she had squeaked too soon. The Lion may have been cowardly, but he wasn't about to let himself be harnessed!

The Witch of the West was no match for the Lion. He was too **STRONG**! Shaking with rage, she slammed the cage closed. "You won't get any food until you obey me!"

DAYS passed, and Dorothy continued to work hard for the wicked Witch. But the Lion still refused to obey.

Every **NIGHT**, in secret, Dorothy and Toto snuck into the Lion's cage to bring him food and **WATER**. Then the three of them curled up together and slept peacefully.

As the days went by, one thought burned in the Witch's mind. Ever since she had laid eyes on Dorothy's enchanted shoes, she wanted nothing more than to put them on her own paws!

One day, the Witch used an invisible walking stick to **TRIP** Dorothy. When Dorothy fell, one of her shoes came off, and the Witch immediately snatched it!

"Give that back!" Dorothy cried, **angrier than a cat in a cage**.

"NEVER — it's mine now!" the Witch replied.

Dorothy had tried to cooperate with the Witch, but this was too much. Without thinking, she grabbed a bucket of WATER and threw it on the Witch. To her surprise, the Witch of the West began to melt right before her eyes! Moldy mozzarella!

Revenge!

Dorothy froze in her fur.

"Swiss cheese on rye!" she squeaked to herself. "What just happened?"

The Witch was furious as she melted like cheese in the sun. "*I'm melting! A powerful witch like me, defeated by a silly little mouse! How horrible!*"

A moment later, nothing remained of the WICKED Witch of the West but a puddle.

Only one thing was left FLOATING in the puddle — the silver shoe.

Dorothy carefully dried it off and put it back on her own paw. Then she and Toto ran to open the Cowardly Lion's cage. They were free!

The poor Winkies were so happy that the wicked Witch of the West was gone, they immediately threw a great party in Dorothy's honor. There was an enormouse amount of singing and *dancing*!

"Oh, if only the Tin Woodman and the Scarecrow were here!" the Lion moaned.

"Maybe we can still save them," Dorothy said. She turned to the Winkies. "Is there a TiNSMiTH among you?"

"Not one — many!" they replied in unison. Several Winkies stepped forward with their tools. "We're ready to help you however we can!"

Dorothy, Toto, and the Lion headed out with the tinsmiths as fast as their paws would take them. They searched high and low for the **ROCKY** plateau where the Flying Monkeys had attacked them. When they arrived, the Woodman was still lying on the rocks, dented and rusting.

The tinsmiths carried him to the CASTLE, examined him carefully, and started fixing him up. Before long, the Tin Woodman was looking better than before! The Winkies even made him a new ax with a golden handle.

Beaming, the Woodman hugged his friends. He couldn't hold back tears! Dorothy rushed to dry them with her apron, worried that the tears would rust his face.

Now they just needed to save the Scarecrow! His clothes had ended up in a tall tree, and his straw had been scattered all over the place.

The Winkies offered to help them

look for their lost friend. The Woodman led the way, walking TALL with his new ax on his shoulder.

They FINALLY reached the tree with the poor Scarecrow's clothes. Rancid ricotta, they were up awfully high!

The Woodman swung his ax, and the tree soon FELL to the ground with a crash. Dorothy and the Winkies gathered the Scarecrow's clothes and brought them back to the castle, where a skilled seamstress filled them with fresh straw. When the seamstress had finished, the Scarecrow jumped back on his feet and bowed to everyone in thanks. He was as good as new!

Now there was only one thing left for the friends to do — return to the Wizard of Oz so that he could keep his promise!

When it was time to say good-bye, the

Revenge!

Winkies gave Toto and the Lion each a golden collar. They gave the Scarecrow a walking stick with a golden head. They presented the Tin Woodman with a silver OILCAN. And they gave Dorothy a fabumouse DiAMOND bracelet.

Dorothy also took the Witch of the West's Golden Cap. She had no idea that it was enchanted, but it was so beautiful that she couldn't leave it behind!

Lost!

There was no straight path between the Witch of the West's **CASTLE** and the Emerald City.

"The only thing to do is to walk east, where the $\mathcal{SUN}$ rises," Dorothy said.

So that's what they did, passing through WOODS and meadows. But by noon, the sun rose high above their heads. They didn't know which direction was east anymore, and they soon lost their way. Cheese niblets, what a **MESS**!

Dorothy tried to keep her snout up. "If we continue on, we'll surely end up somewhere!"

The friends kept walking, but days passed with no trace of the Emerald City. Before long, they were all so exhausted they could hardly squeak!

"We're lost!" the Scarecrow moaned. "Now we'll never get back to the Emerald City, and I'll never get my brain!"

"I'll never get a heart!" the poor Tin Woodman cried.

"And I'll be a coward forever!" the Lion roared.

Disheartened, Dorothy sunk down onto the GRASS. Suddenly, she remembered something — the whistle from the Queen of the Rabbits! This was the perfect time to try it out.

As soon as Dorothy BLEW on the whistle, LIGHT pawsteps moved the grass around them, until . . . cheesy cream puffs! The Rabbits appeared out of nowhere with their Queen!

Dorothy explained their problem.

"You went the wrong direction, and now the Emerald City is very far away," the Queen explained. "But you could use the GOLDEN CAP . . ."

"Golden Cap?" Dorothy replied, confused.

"Of course! With *that* hat," the Queen said, pointing to Dorothy's head, "you can summon the famouse Flying Monkeys! You can call on them three times, and they must obey your orders. Anyone in Oz would love to have the Golden Cap."

HOLEY CHEESE! Dorothy had no idea the beautiful hat was so powerful!

Then the Queen added, "If you do call the Monkeys, we'll leave now so that we don't have to deal with their usual PRANKS."

Dorothy thanked the kind Rabbits, and they scampered away.

Lost!

When the five friends were alone again, Dorothy took the Golden Cap off her head and noticed that there were some FUNNY words and instructions sewn inside. "Well, it can't hurt to try," she murmured.

With that, she put the Golden Cap back on her head and repeated the magic words. She stood on her left paw, then the right, then on both, and squeaked:

"Ep-pe, pep-pe, kak-ke!
Hil-lo, hol-lo, hel-lo!
Ziz-zy, zuz-zy, zik!"

A moment later, the thundering wings of the Flying Monkeys echoed throughout the meadow. Once they landed, the chief bowed to Dorothy. "What do you command, mistress?"

Dorothy took a deep breath. She tried to be **brave**, but it was hard to face the same monkeys who had hurt and captured them before! "Take us to the Emerald City, please," she squeaked. "We must see the great Oz!"

The Monkeys gently took Dorothy and her friends by the arms and LiFTeD them into the air. Double-twisted rattails, what a view! Less than an hour later, the little group was back inside the Emerald City.

The Wizard's Trick

The Guardian of the city greeted the group with an astounded look on his snout.

"Crusty cat litter! Weren't you supposed to find the Witch of the West?" he asked.

"Yes!" Dorothy said, BEAMING. "We found her — and we defeated her!"

"The Witch was defeated?!" he squeaked. "This is truly fabumouse news!"

When the Guardian spread the word that Dorothy and her friends had destroyed the Witch of the West, the mice of the Emerald City all crowded around them, cheering and celebrating as they made their way to Oz's palace.

But a bitter surprise was waiting at the palace — the Wizard did not want to see them! Rotten rat's teeth! How could Oz refuse to see them? He had a PROMISE to keep!

Days went by. Finally, the Scarecrow turned to one of the Wizard's servants.

"Tell the Wizard if he doesn't see us soon, we'll call the **Flying Monkeys** to his palace!" the Scarecrow said.

Cheese and crackers, the Scarecrow's plan worked! The great Wizard immediately called for the five friends to come to the throne room together. They weren't sure what to expect, since the Wizard had appeared different to each of them before. What would he look like now? To their surprise, the throne room was completely EMPTY.

For the love of cheese, where was he?

Dorothy, Toto, the Scarecrow, the Tin Woodman, and the Lion waited *silently*. Finally, a loud voice **BOOMED**.

"I am the great and terrible Oz! Who are you? And why have you come to see me?"

Dorothy and her friends exchanged confused looks. "Who are we?" the Woodman burst out. "It's **US**! We've come to claim the things you promised!"

The Wizard's **VOICE** was silent. Then he murmured, "Is it true that you have defeated the Witch of the West?"

"Of course it's true," Dorothy said. "We would never **LIE**!"

Frustrated, the Cowardly Lion roared so loudly that Toto **JUMPED** with fear, knocking over the little screen that covered one corner of the room.

CHEESE NIBLETS — the group of friends couldn't believe their eyes! In that very corner was a tiny, bald, wrinkly man with an embarrassed look on his face.

"Who are YOU?" the Tin Woodman asked.

"I — I am Oz, the g-great and t-terrible Oz . . ." the man replied, shaking.

Dorothy and her friends stared at him in disbelief. Holey cheese! That **wrinkly**, trembling little man couldn't be Oz!

"Don't **HARM** me, please!" he begged. "I'm just an ordinary man. I've . . . I've tricked you." He hung his head in shame.

Dorothy twisted her tail. "TRICKED? You mean . . . you're not a great wizard?"

"No," the man said meekly. "I'm not a wizard at all."

"No, you're not!" the Scarecrow cried. "You're a **crook**!"

"That's right." The man nodded. "But a very skilled crook, you have to admit. I have an **ENTIRE** kingdom obeying me, even though I don't have a cheese crumb of magical power!"

"But I don't understand," Dorothy said. "How could you appear in so many different forms?"

"I used TRICKS," he explained. "Here, I'll show you."

With that, he led them into a **SECRET** room . . .

The Secrets of
the Great Oz

Oz's secret room contained many marvemouse things, including circus equipment, magician's props, and costumes. There was the giant head that Dorothy had seen during her first visit, which was made of papier-mâché; costumes for the fairy and the wild beast that had fooled the Scarecrow and the Tin Woodman; and an enormouse cotton ball, which had been used to light the FIRE during the Lion's visit.

"Long ago," Oz explained, "I learned how to do ventriloquism: I would speak with my mouth closed, and make it sound like my voice was coming from somewhere else. I started performing, and extended my act to include magic tricks. Then I learned to fly a hot air balloon and took to the sky! But one day, I lost control of the balloon and ended up here. Mice saw me DESCEND from the clouds and thought that I must be a wizard. So I went along with it. With all the TRICKS I knew, it was easy cheesy!"

Dorothy and her friends listened, curious and outraged.

"I had the Emerald City built," the Wizard continued, "and made everyone wear glasses with green lenses. But everything only appears green because you're wearing the glasses! As the years went on, I let everyone spread rumors about my fabumouse magic, and tried to keep out of sight."

The five friends looked at Oz in disbelief. Slimy Swiss balls, what a horrible TRICK!

Oz continued, "I was afraid of only two rodents: the Witch of the East and the Witch of the West. But now that they have both been **defeated**, I'm sorry to say that I can't keep my promises to you. I have no powers!"

Dorothy crossed her arms angrily. "For such a small thing, you're an awfully BIG rat! What are we going to do?"

"I demand my brain!" the Scarecrow cried.

"You don't need one, though!" Oz replied. "Experience is what makes you intelligent, and you've already had more adventures than most creatures have in a lifetime."

"And what about my courage?" the Cowardly Lion roared.

Oz smiled. "Every living thing is afraid of facing DANGER. True courage is facing danger even when you're afraid. It seems to me that you already know how to do that!"

The Tin Woodman spoke up next. "Now I suppose you'll tell me that I already have a heart!"

Oz's reply wasn't what they expected. "Well, no — but that might not be such a bad thing. Believe me: A heart can bring you great joy, but it can also make you suffer!"

"What about me?" Dorothy said. "You must help me get home — you promised!"

The mouse sighed. "I don't know if I can help any of you, but come back tomorrow and I'll see what I can do. In the meantime, please don't tell anyone that I'm not a real **wizard**, or I'll be ruined!"

"That would serve you right," the Woodman said sternly. "But we still need your help, so we'll keep to ourselves. Besides, I think you'll see that when you trick people, you end up being the one in **trouble**!"

The next day, Dorothy and her friends all visited Oz again, separately this time. The Scarecrow was the first to enter the throne room.

Oz asked him to sit down, and **gently** pulled off the Scarecrow's head. He took it into his secret room and filled it with bran, pins, and needles. He shook it well, and then put the head back in place on the Scarecrow's body.

"Now you have the finest **brain** in all the land!" the man declared.

Thrilled, the Scarecrow thanked him and proudly returned to his friends.

"How do you feel?" Dorothy asked him.

"Very wise!" he replied with a grin.

Next, the Tin Woodman entered the throne room to receive his heart.

Oz took a pair of steel scissors and cut a rectangular WINDOW in the Woodman's chest. Then he opened a box and took out a small silver heart.

"Oh, how beautiful!" the Woodman cried as soon as he saw it.

Oz placed it in his chest, closed the window, and welded it back together.

The Woodman left with a joyful spring in his step. He sent in the Cowardly Lion.

This time, Oz opened a wardrobe and pulled out a green bottle. He emptied the contents into a bowl and handed it to the Lion, who sniffed the liquid with a confused expression on his snout.

"Drink!" Oz urged him. "Once you swallow this, it will turn into courage!"

Without hesitating, the Lion gulped down the strange syrup and raced back to his friends, feeling more courageous than ever.

Alone in the throne room, Oz rubbed his hands together with satisfaction. It hadn't been hard to help with those first three wishes!

But now he had to face Dorothy. Rats — he was in trouble!

Up, Up, and Away!

Dorothy had to **wait** for three days before Oz finally called her back to the throne room. She felt like tearing out her whiskers!

"I believe I've found a solution," the **man** finally announced. "I can't guarantee that we'll get back to Kansas . . . but we'll try."

Dorothy was **STUNNED**. "*We'll* try?" she repeated. "Are you coming, too?"

The little man nodded. "I'm tired of fooling everyone. I will come with you. Surely I can find work at a circus somewhere!"

Dorothy smiled. Oz wasn't a **BAD** man after all — he was just a **BAD** wizard!

Oz rubbed his paws together and explained his plan. "As you know, I flew here in a HOT AIR BALLOON. So we'll leave in one, too!"

It was a fabumouse idea! The pair immediately got to work building a hot air balloon, since Oz's original balloon had long since been destroyed. Oz had several strips of green silk brought in, and Dorothy helped sew them together. It took three long days of work. But when they were finished, they had an enormouse silk balloon!

Oz carefully brushed the balloon all over with glue to make it waterproof. Then he used thick ropes to attach it to a huge, flat-bottomed basket that had been hanging in his secret room. Finally, he **ORDERED** his servants to bring the balloon to the front of the palace so everyone could admire it. It was truly a marvemouse sight!

The Woodman chopped a pile of wood, stacked it carefully under the silk balloon, and lit a **FIRE**. The balloon captured the **HOT AIR**, and it swelled up. Luckily, it was anchored to the ground with **strong** ropes!

When Oz, Dorothy, and Toto were ready to begin their journey, Oz put on a large, elaborate cloak that covered him from head to toe. It hid his true form so the mice who gathered at the palace didn't realize he was a liar.

"Subjects!" he **proclaimed**. "I am

leaving to visit a wizard friend of mine who lives far, far away. I am appointing the Scarecrow to govern this kingdom. I **ORDER** you to obey him as you would obey me!"

With that, Oz jumped into the balloon's basket. Dorothy and Toto were about to do the same, when —

CRRRRACK!

The ropes holding the hot air balloon to the ground broke, and the balloon floated away without Dorothy and Toto!

"I'm sorry, my dear!" Oz squeaked from above. "But I can't turn back now! Farewell and **good luck**!"

And with that, the Wizard of Oz sailed off into the sky, leaving a ʃqueaᴋleʃʃ Dorothy behind.

The Land of the Quadlings

Dorothy was **determined** to find a way to return to Kansas.

So she put on the GOLDEN CAP and called the Flying Monkeys for the second time. Unfortunately, they couldn't take her outside the realm of Oz. Rat-munching rattlesnakes!

The guard with the long GREEN beard suggested that she go see Glinda, the Witch of the South, in the Land of the Quadlings. She would surely be able to help!

Her friends went along — even the Scarecrow, who had just been proclaimed KING of Oz.

"There will be plenty of time to rule," he said wisely. "Dorothy needs me now!"

They walked a long way, through a forest of TREES that grabbed at their clothes. Squeak, how terrifying! Luckily, the Tin Woodman chopped off some BRANCHES and cleared a path.

When they got out of the forest, they found themselves in a strange land where everything was made of china . . . including the rodents!

Everything was so **tiny** and fragile. The group moved very carefully. They didn't want to destroy anything — or anyone!

Cheese and crackers, what a strange place!

Next, Dorothy and her friends reached a dark forest where hundreds of beasts were having a meeting! They explained that an enormouse MONSTER had been terrorizing them for months. Without a moment to waste, the Lion defeated the monster with great courage, like a real King of the Forest. The beasts were so grateful!

Dorothy and her friends continued along, barely escaping an attack by some strange creatures called Hammer-Heads. Finally, Dorothy decided to call the Flying Monkeys for the third and final time.

"Take us to the Land of the Quadlings!" she COMMANDED.

And they did!

The Quadlings were small and PLUMP rodents, dressed in scarlet from head to tail! They led Dorothy and her friends to Glinda, the Witch of the South. She was young and beautiful, with thick ruby-red hair.

"If I'm going to send you home, I'll need

the wicked Witch of the West's GOLDEN CAP," she said kindly to Dorothy.

Dorothy pawed it over immediately. After all, the hat was no use to her anymore!

"Very good," Glinda said with a smile. "I will use it to send your friends to the places where they will be happiest: the Scarecrow to the Emerald City, where he has been proclaimed king; the Tin Woodman to the land of the Winkies, where he has been elected as their leader; and the Lion to the FOREST, where he will rule over the beasts. Then I'll give the Golden Cap back to the chief of the Flying Monkeys, so they will be free. And as for you, my dear . . ."

Home Again!

Dorothy hung on every word spoken by the Witch of the South.

"To return home, use the silver shoes on your paws," Glinda explained. "They are enchanted, and they will take you wherever you like! Just TAP the heels together three times. Then squeak the name of the place you want to go."

Dorothy's eyes **WIDENED** in disbelief. She could have gone home ages ago! But then she wouldn't have had all those fabumouse adventures with her incredible new friends!

With this in mind, Dorothy turned to her faithful friends to say good-bye!

She threw her arms around the Lion's neck, smacked a **kiss** on the Woodman's tin cheek, and hugged the Scarecrow tightly.

"Good-bye, my friends!" she squeaked, tears rolling down her snout.

The Lion, Tin Woodman, and Scarecrow all waved sadly. "We'll never forget you!" they cried.

Dorothy took Toto in her arms, thanked the Witch of the South, and tapped her heels together three times. "*Take me home!*" she squeaked.

Suddenly, she found herself spinning in the air. A moment later, she TUMBLED onto the GRASS next to a small house. Dorothy realized that this was the farmhouse Uncle Henry had built after the old one had been carried off by the tornado.

Holey cheese — she was finally **home**!

Dorothy glanced down at her paws. The silver shoes were gone, but Dorothy didn't have time to miss them. Just then Aunt Em came out the front door!

Dorothy ran to meet her, beaming. "Aunt Em! I'm back! I'm home again!"

Aunt Em was completely squeakless! She looked at Dorothy in shock — and then a smile stretched across her snout as she wrapped Dorothy up in an enormouse hug. She had given up hope of ever seeing Dorothy again.

"I can't believe it!" Aunt Em cried, smoothing Dorothy's fur and straightening her whiskers.

Dorothy squeezed her aunt tightly. She could hardly believe it, too! With a contented smile, she whispered, "I'm so happy to be home."

L. Frank Baum

Lyman Frank Baum was born in 1856 to a prosperous family in Chittenango, New York. When he was a teenager, his father bought him a small printing press. Using this basic tool, he printed his first amateur newspaper. Then he printed another and another. Before long, he became interested in the theater, where he could truly let his imagination run wild!

Baum discovered that on the stage, his craziest stories could come to life! He was determined to make all his dreams come true — to be a writer, to work in a theater, and to produce great musicals. He held many different jobs throughout his life in order to make money. He was a reporter, a shopkeeper, and even a chicken farmer! Eventually, he was able to dedicate himself to the theater as an actor, producer, and scriptwriter.

In 1882, he married Maud Gage and moved to South Dakota. They had four sons together. In 1900, he published *The Wonderful Wizard of Oz*, which was inspired by a story he had made up for his children and neighbors. The book was a fantastic success, and Baum went on to publish thirteen more novels set in the world of Oz. He even transformed the first story into a successful musical. He died in Glendale, California, in 1919.

ABOUT THE AUTHOR

Born in New Mouse City, Mouse Island, **GERONIMO STILTON** is Rattus Emeritus of Mousomorphic Literature and of Neo-Ratonic Comparative Philosophy. For the past twenty years, he has been running *The Rodent's Gazette*, New Mouse City's most widely read daily newspaper.

Stilton was awarded the Ratitzer Prize for his scoops on *The Curse of the Cheese Pyramid* and *The Search for Sunken Treasure*. He has also received the Andersen 2000 Prize for Personality of the Year. One of his bestsellers won the 2002 eBook Award for world's best ratlings' electronic book. His works have been published all over the globe.

In his spare time, Mr. Stilton collects antique cheese rinds and plays golf. But what he most enjoys is telling stories to his nephew Benjamin.

Be sure to read all my fabumouse adventures!

#1 Lost Treasure of the Emerald Eye

#2 The Curse of the Cheese Pyramid

#3 Cat and Mouse in a Haunted House

#4 I'm Too Fond of My Fur!

#5 Four Mice Deep in the Jungle

#6 Paws Off, Cheddarface!

#7 Red Pizzas for a Blue Count

#8 Attack of the Bandit Cats

#9 A Fabumouse Vacation for Geronimo

#10 All Because of a Cup of Coffee

#11 It's Halloween, You 'Fraidy Mouse!

#12 Merry Christmas, Geronimo!

#13 The Phantom of the Subway

#14 The Temple of the Ruby of Fire

#15 The Mona Mousa Code

#16 A Cheese-Colored Camper

#17 Watch Your Whiskers, Stilton!

#18 Shipwreck on the Pirate Islands

#19 My Name Is Stilton, Geronimo Stilton

#20 Surf's Up, Geronimo!

#21 The Wild, Wild West

#22 The Secret of Cacklefur Castle

A Christmas Tale

#23 Valentine's Day Disaster

#24 Field Trip to Niagara Falls

#25 The Search for Sunken Treasure

#26 The Mummy with No Name

#27 The Christmas Toy Factory

#28 Wedding Crasher

#29 Down and Out Down Under

#30 The Mouse Island Marathon

#31 The Mysterious Cheese Thief

Christmas Catastrophe

#32 Valley of the Giant Skeletons

#33 Geronimo and the Gold Medal Mystery

#34 Geronimo Stilton, Secret Agent

#35 A Very Merry Christmas

#36 Geronimo's Valentine

#37 The Race Across America

#38 A Fabumouse School Adventure

#39 Singing Sensation

#40 The Karate Mouse

#41 Mighty Mount Kilimanjaro

#42 The Peculiar Pumpkin Thief

#43 I'm Not a Supermouse!

#44 The Giant Diamond Robbery

#45 Save the White Whale!

#46 The Haunted Castle

#47 Run for the Hills,
Geronimo!

#48 The Mystery in
Venice

#49 The Way of
the Samurai

#50 This Hotel Is
Haunted!

#51 The Enormouse
Pearl Heist

#52 Mouse in Space!

#53 Rumble in
the Jungle

#54 Get into Gear,
Stilton!

#55 The Golden
Statue Plot

#56 Flight of the
Red Bandit

The Hunt for the
Golden Book

#57 The Stinky
Cheese Vacation

#58 The Super
Chef Contest

#59 Welcome to
Moldy Manor

The Hunt for the
Curious Cheese

#60 The Treasure of
Easter Island

#61 Mouse House
Hunter

#62 Mouse
Overboard!

The Hunt for the
Secret Papyrus

#63 The Cheese
Experiment

#64 Magical Mission

#65 Bollywood
Burglary

The Hunt for the
Hundredth Key

Don't miss any of my special edition adventures!

THE KINGDOM OF FANTASY

THE QUEST FOR PARADISE:
THE RETURN TO THE KINGDOM OF FANTASY

THE AMAZING VOYAGE:
THE THIRD ADVENTURE IN THE KINGDOM OF FANTASY

THE DRAGON PROPHECY:
THE FOURTH ADVENTURE IN THE KINGDOM OF FANTASY

THE VOLCANO OF FIRE:
THE FIFTH ADVENTURE IN THE KINGDOM OF FANTASY

THE SEARCH FOR TREASURE:
THE SIXTH ADVENTURE IN THE KINGDOM OF FANTASY

THE ENCHANTED CHARMS:
THE SEVENTH ADVENTURE IN THE KINGDOM OF FANTASY

THE PHOENIX OF DESTINY:
AN EPIC KINGDOM OF FANTASY ADVENTURE

THE HOUR OF MAGIC:
THE EIGHTH ADVENTURE IN THE KINGDOM OF FANTASY

THE WIZARD'S WAND:
THE NINTH ADVENTURE IN THE KINGDOM OF FANTASY

THE JOURNEY THROUGH TIME

BACK IN TIME:
THE SECOND JOURNEY THROUGH TIME

THE RACE AGAINST TIME:
THE THIRD JOURNEY THROUGH TIME

LOST IN TIME:
THE FOURTH JOURNEY THROUGH TIME

MEET GERONIMO STILTONIX

He is a spacemouse — the Geronimo Stilton of a parallel universe! He is captain of the spaceship *MouseStar 1*. While flying through the cosmos, he visits distant planets and meets crazy aliens. His adventures are out of this world!

#1 Alien Escape

#2 You're Mine, Captain!

#3 Ice Planet Adventure

#4 The Galactic Goal

#5 Rescue Rebellion

#6 The Underwater Planet

#7 Beware! Space Junk!

#8 Away in a Star Sled

#9 Slurp Monster Showdown

#10 Pirate Spacecat Attack

MEET
Geronimo Stiltonord

He is a mouseking — the Geronimo Stilton of the ancient far north! He lives with his brawny and brave clan in the village of Mouseborg. From sailing frozen waters to facing fiery dragons, every day is an adventure for the micekings!

#1 Attack of the Dragons

#2 The Famouse Fjord Race

#3 Pull the Dragon's Tooth!

#4 Stay Strong, Geronimo!

Dear mouse friends,
Thanks for reading, and farewell
till the next book.
It'll be another whisker-licking-good
adventure, and that's a promise!

Geronimo Stilton